Nefertiti & Ramses

Coloring Book

T.L. Johnson

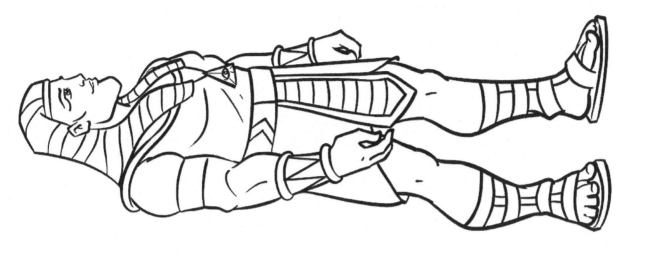
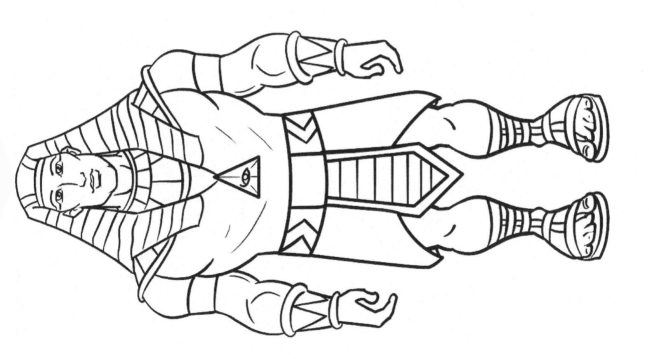

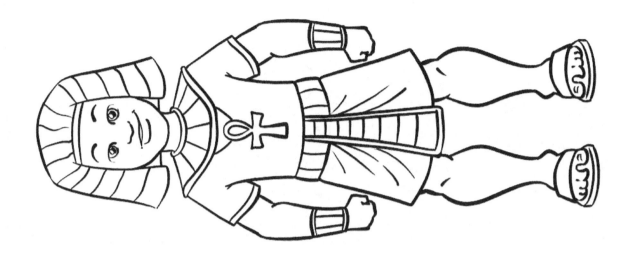
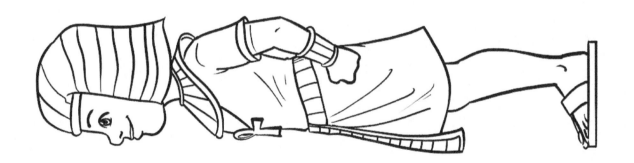

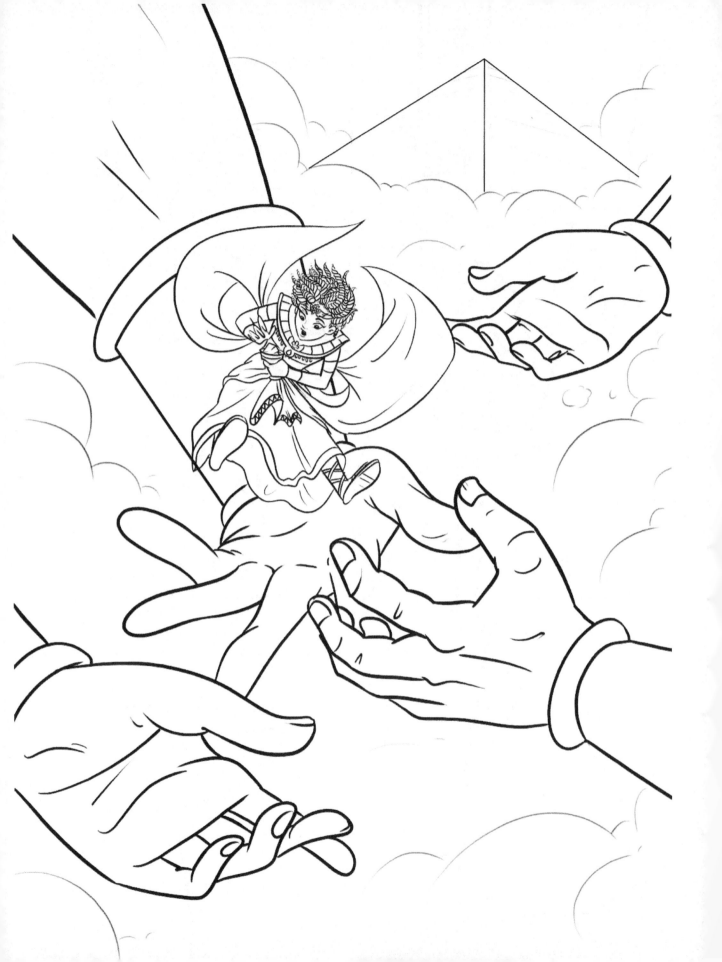

NEFERTITI AND THE GREAT LAKE

THE GREAT LAKE

NERFITIT AND THE GREAT LAKE

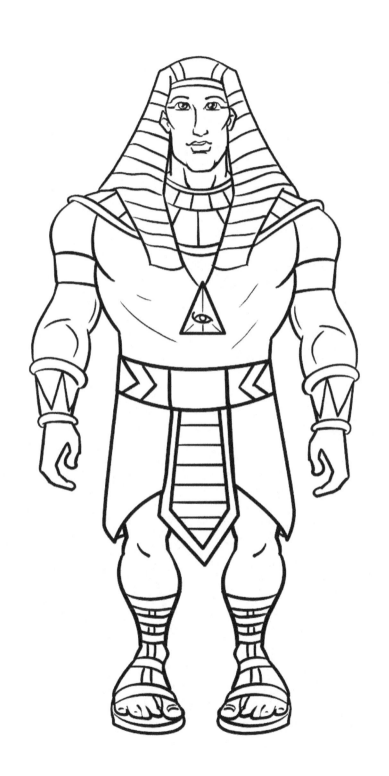

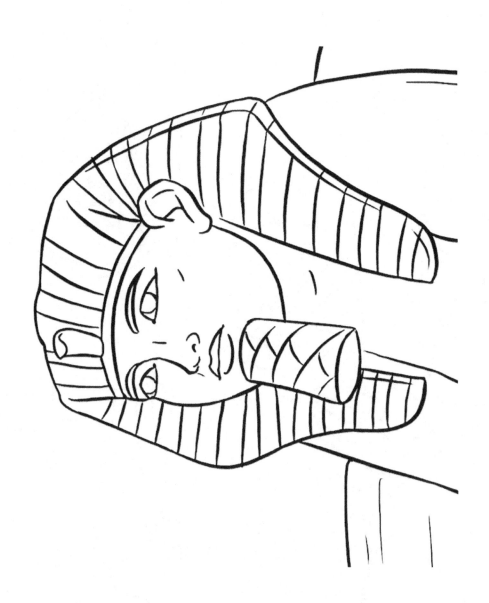

3

THE GREAT SAGE

NEFERTITI

FRIENDS

FOREVER

Made in United States
Orlando, FL
29 November 2021